Power Armor for Poltergeists!

Simon Christiansen

ISBN: 978-87-94505-01-7

DEDICATION

This story is dedicated to all those readers who write reviews on Amazon, Goodreads, and similar sites.

Your support means the world to us writers.

CONTENTS

ACKNOWLEDGMENTS

I would like to thank my family, friends, and readers, who gave me invaluable support and feedback during the writing of this book.

The three poems following the story were previously published by poetry journals. I would therefore like to acknowledge:

Cosmic Daffodil Journal, which published *Submarine Salvation*, *Graphic Violence Lit*, which published *Starfish*, and *Dreams & Nightmares*, the publisher of *Apoequorin*.

POWER ARMOR FOR POLTERGEISTS!

"Power armor for poltergeists will become the next great fad in consumer electronics!" said Dr. Birk. He combed back his white hair with his hand and studied my reaction with bright blue eyes like sapphires. His lab coat fit like a tuxedo.

I considered the sparkling machines, the intricate robotic arms sprouting from the walls, and the comforting smell of ozone. All in service to the tall, bulky suit of military-grade power armor occupying the corner of the lab.

"Consider the humble Ouija board," continued the doctor. "Tiny perturbations in the planchette are subconsciously amplified by the participants, causing it to traverse the board with surprising alacrity."

I was beginning to regret my choice of postdoc project.

"I thought this was a robotics lab."

"And how are robots controlled, Mr. Vinther? Imagine a control interface using feedback mechanisms that amplify tiny movements before sending them to the processing unit, just like the hands of the participants amplify the shivers of the planchette."

He poured himself a cup of coffee, and the nutty, caramel

aroma made the lab feel more homely. "You must understand the importance of the research we do here. Our ancestors and loved ones are the sources of our selves. To reconnect with them is to reconnect with our natures. Throughout history, the search for meaning has gone hand in hand with the attempt to reconnect with the dead. Coffee?"

We sipped our coffee. "Why power armor, though? Wouldn't some kind of mannequin be more relatable?"

The doctor shook his head. "It's the uncanny valley. Attempting to recreate a dead person's face and body becomes creepy and disconcerting. A big, hulking suit of power armor allows people to imagine that their loved ones are inside, piloting the suit, as indeed they are. Besides, the feedback actuators are too big to fit into anything smaller."

He walked over to the suit of armor and patted the arm; shiny metal distorted his face like a funhouse mirror.

"Aren't poltergeists angry spirits lashing out, though? I thought consenting spirits should pilot these suits."

He raised an eyebrow. "Surely, you're not one of those pharisaical philistines who value semantics over proper alliteration? One must consider marketing!

"I must confess I had ulterior motives for hiring you. We will need a strong spirit to power the first set of armor, one driven by strong emotions. I understand that the late Mrs. Vinther…."

I froze; my hands clenched, and nails pierced my palms. Pain. "No."

"Mr. Vinther…"

"I'm not using my ex-wife as fuel for your insane contraption!"

"Fuel? Far from it! She will wear the armor like a wedding dress of chrome and steel!"

I punched him in the face, and the nails dug deeper into my palm. Blood tickled the skin. He toppled over from the force.

"That's what I am talking about," he said from the floor, sputtering as blood from his nose ran rivulets into his mouth. "Energy! I'm not unfamiliar with grief."

Of course. The doctor's wife, mother, and two children had died at Linköping. He had thrown himself into his work after that. The pain in my palms subsided as my hands relaxed.

"Let me make you a proposition," said the doctor. "Why not let your wife decide for herself? We'll use an old-fashioned Ouija board with no mechanical amplifiers."

With a sweep of his arm, he cleared an area on the central table, boards, and tools, and doodads clattering against each other. He fetched a Ouija board from a shelf and plopped it on the table.

"Grab on!"

Fine. I sighed and placed my hands on the planchette. A cloud passed over the sun outside, and the room darkened, the gleaming chrome of walls, table, and armor turning a dull grey.

"Maria Vinther," he intoned. "Your husband misses you dearly and wishes to speak with you. If you share his wish, make your presence known!"

The air grew colder; the planchette jerked and then darted across the board, visiting each letter in turn.

"KRISTIAN? IS THAT YOU? WHAT TOOK YOU SO LONG?"

"Maria…" I whispered. "I thought I needed to let you rest…"

"OH, FUCK THAT. DO YOU KNOW HOW BORING IT IS TO 'REST'? THERE'S NOTHING TO DO HERE. WHAT ARE YOU UP TO?"

"I…" I began, but the doctor interrupted me. "You two

lovebirds can catch up later. Mrs. Vinther, your strength is remarkable. I am Doctor Birk, and I have a proposition for you."

The doorbell buzzed, and I withdrew my hands from the planchette. Light returned to the laboratory. The doctor swore. I turned as the steel entrance door slid into the wall with a pneumatic hiss.

A tall woman strode into the room. Dark-blonde hair stopped at the edge of her shoulders, curling upwards like waves striking land. Her white lab coat was identical to the doctor's, and an oval black eye patch adorned her left eye.

Behind her, a short man with a clipboard and a dark suit followed and started taking notes. For a moment, the sound of pencil on paper was all that broke the silence.

"Dr. Vestergaard," said Dr. Birk. "Always a pleasure."

"Of course, it isn't." she sneered. "A little bird tells me you are working on a project." She nodded towards the suit of armor.

Dr. Birk smiled a frozen joyless smile. "I assume the little bird is my previous postdoc, Mr. Dahl."

"Don't act surprised, doctor. Not everyone shares your disdain for civic duty. Mr. Dahl realized that your projects would do more good in the hands of the glorious Danish welfare state. You should be proud of him."

She pivoted on her heel to face me and extended her hand. A card stuck between manicured fingernails; instinctively, I took it.

"Dr. Vestergaard

Ministry of Esoteric Development."

"The doctor wishes to monetize your grief. We would use it in service of the welfare state. The Ministry is adept at turning asinine research into public utility."

"If you're so good with technology, why are you wearing an eyepatch?"

"It's the uncanny valley. People find my bionic eye creepy, so I cover it with a patch and crank up the sensitivity to see through it. I have flawless depth perception."

She turned and strode through the doorway without waiting for an answer. The man with the clipboard followed, scribbling furiously, and the metal door slid into place.

The doctor shook his head. "The welfare state has its uses, but planning scientific research is not one of them. As part of my company, you'll help make decisions directly!"

He padded me on the shoulder. "Look, why don't you go home and think? Your late wife wouldn't want you to rush the decision."

***

Sara had made Keshi Yena, a Caribbean dish consisting of a great ball of cheese stuffed with spicy meat. The invigorating smell of cheese and spices filled the air. She sat on the other side of the table. Her familiar, freckled face and ruffled auburn hair.

"Is something on your mind, honey?"

I had been poking the yellow ball on my plate for several minutes without eating.

I told her about my day.

She was silent for a while, poking her ball with fork and knife. A bit of spicy chicken meat spilled from the wound onto the plate.

"You still miss her? Sorry, what a dumb question. I'm not expecting you to forget her. I mean, do you want to talk to her?"

"I'm not sure… Of course, I knew that ghosts existed. For some reason, I never imagined Maria would be the kind of person to stick around. I always figured she would be off on a new adventure, wherever they go."

She put her hand on mine. The warmth of blood and life. "You can talk to her if you want. Don't worry. I won't feel threatened by a dead woman."

"Not even if she's piloting a two-and-a-half-meter-tall suit of military-grade power armor?"

She laughed. "You're hardly going to tap that, are you?"

I laughed.

"Okay, I'll tell the doctor I'm in. I always thought you and Maria would've made great friends."

She skewered the ball, causing steaming meat to spill onto the plate. The aroma of spice and cheese made my mouth water.

***

The doctor waited for me in the lab in the morning. He poured me a cup of coffee and clinked his mug against mine as if celebrating with champagne. Hot and black. He offered neither milk nor sugar.

"I knew you would come around," he said. "Let me show you the future home of Mrs. Vinther."

He pressed a button, and a wall section slid into the ceiling with a pneumatic hiss, revealing a two-and-a-half-meter tall gleaming suit of power armor lit by fluorescent lights.

I put my sunglasses on.

"I spent all night polishing it," said the doctor. "Literally as well as figuratively. I removed the weaponry, but the exterior is otherwise identical to the military model. Besides, we can always reattach the bazooka once I've gotten to know your wife."

"The next part is up to you," he continued. "Put your hand on the armor's surface and summon her!"

The surface was cool and slick to the touch. I took a deep breath and spoke: "Maria. It's me, Kristian. If you can hear me, come into this armor, and return to the world of the living."

The entire suit shuddered, and the smooth metal surface rubbed against my palm, friction warming the skin. The armor emerged from the enclosure onto the lab floor with a single humongous step. Every side now shone in the light from the windows.

Slowly, the armor raised both arms and spread the fingers wide. Another shudder went through the length of the suit. Both arms dropped to the sides, and a synthetic voice issued from the grating in the helmet.

"KRISTIAN? I'VE MISSED HAVING ARMS TO STRETCH!"

"Does the synthetic voice have to be so generic?" I whispered to the doctor.

"It's the uncanny valley," he whispered back. "If I tried to make it sound like your wife, it would be creepy and weird. This way, your imagination can fill in the blanks!"

"I'M STANDING RIGHT HERE!"

"I'm sorry, honey." I reached out and put my right hand in one of her giant palms. She scooped me up, and before I knew what had happened, I sat on her shoulder, my hair brushing against the ceiling.

"HA! I'M NOT GONNA BE SITTING ON YOUR LAP ANYMORE, THAT'S FOR SURE."

"The yellow knob controls the volume," said the doctor.

"LIKE This," she said. "Is that better?"

"Much better, honey," I said, removing my hand from my ear and stabilizing myself on her iron arm. "Uh… How have you been?"

She stepped forward, and I grabbed her shoulder to keep my balance. "Well, dead, you know. I floated among the trees, trying to become one with nature. I was always more of an Eastern girl, so it felt more natural than looking for a tunnel of light or whateverthefuck."

"Yet, here you are," I said and smiled at the grating in the helmet, imagining her face inside.

"HA! Yeah, whenever I started to drift away, I would think about what you were up to, and it would pull me back."

"There's something I should tell…"

"Ha, don't worry, I'm not gonna haunt that chick, whatshername, the cook, Sara! I know I'm dead, and she isn't."

The doctor had been staring enraptured but now emerged from his reverie. "Well, Mr. and Mrs. Vinther, why don't the two of you take the armor for a test drive? I want to get this technology to market as soon as possible."

I opened my mouth, but Maria was faster. "Sure! I can't wait to see what you've done with the place!"

The armor dashed toward the door, and I grabbed hold of the back of her head. The metal was cool, but gusts of air emerged from the helmet. I imagined Maria inside, wearing her favorite dress, pulling levers and pressing buttons, with her trademark cheeky smile.

On the way home, I handed out brochures to onlookers and dropped a few beside a homeless man sleeping on a bench.

***

When we arrived, Sara stood in the doorway, staring open-mouthed at our approach. Her hair glowed in the sunlight; the armor sparkled; I smiled and jumped to the porch, and the smell of spices from the kitchen tickled my nose.

Sara spoke first. "Good afternoon, Mrs. Vinther. I've heard so much about you."

"Ha! You don't have to call me that. That was only till death did us part. I'm Maria Beck, again."

"And I'm Sara Thorn."

Sara had set the table in the front yard. Three plates of steaming hot pasta with crimson sauce. "Aw, you didn't need to get a plate for me," said Maria.

Nearby people gathered in their yards, watching the armor with wide, curious eyes. I could not help but consider marketing. Sara and I enjoyed the pasta while Maria watched, her plate untouched. Unable to eat herself, Maria fed us her food, carefully manipulating the cutlery with giant hands so that pasta descended into our mouths.

Maria's new body was too large and heavy for the house. I hugged her leg and said goodnight. Cool metal in my arms.

Later, through the bedroom window, I saw the armor in the yard, reflecting the moon. Slight movement in the fingers showed that Maria was still playing with the controls.

I drifted off into sleep and dreamt of piano-playing poltergeists.

***

We had breakfast together in the front yard in the cool morning air. Pancakes and scrambled eggs. The smell of strong coffee. Maria positioned herself so that her body reflected the sun, warming us from two sides.

At the doctor's lab building, we marched into the

warehouse, an imposing hall filled with technological wonders. Stacked in rows along the wall, every possible model and permutation. Some were humanoid, like Maria's current shell, but others displayed more arcane forms. In some, there were only a few deviations from the human shape: Tank treads in place of legs; missile launchers instead of arms; two heads, for some reason. Others had no discernible form: Escherian collections of machinery, claws, weapons, and manipulators.

A few moved around, but most stood in formation along the walls; terracotta soldiers waiting for their emperor's return.

The doctor stepped out from behind a suit, a screwdriver in each hand. "There you are," he said, beaming up at Maria and me. "How was the test drive, Mrs. Vinther?"

"Amazing!" she replied. "It feels great to have limbs again. I used to be an aerobics instructor, you know. Being a disembodied spirit was hard to get used to."

I looked at the impressive array of armors lined up against the walls. "I had no idea there were so many models. How did you afford all this?"

The doctor drummed his screwdrivers on the legs of a nearby suit, playing a happy little tune. "Let's say I'm not the only one who sees the commercial potential. Some designs were abandoned as unsuitable for human pilots, but spirits are more versatile. We must figure out the best way to reach our customers."

"Excuse me," said a voice by the gate. The homeless man. In one hand, he held the bag with his earthly possessions; in the other, he brandished the brochure. "I'm Martin. I found this by my bench."

***

He left an hour later, his late, ten-year-old son ensconced in a model with impressive tank treads instead of legs. It crunched twigs and dry leaves as it made its way along the street. Steel arms hugged Martin, who hung from them with his legs swinging.

"DADDY," said the voice of the boy who had not yet learned to operate the volume controls. "WHERE ARE WE GOING?"

"Let's go play ball, son," said Martin. Even from a distance, I could see the sunlight twinkling in his tears.

The doctor slapped me on the back. "Perfect! If that doesn't move armors, I'll eat my hat! Charity and marketing combined!"

Word spread like will-o'-the-wisps. Martin gave people rides on his son's shoulders, and they marveled at the loud, synthetic voice. It wasn't long before crowds formed outside the doctor's lab, and the phones rang around the clock.

Old Mrs. Peterson had lost Mr. Peterson at Linköping. We put him in a standard humanoid model with retractable skating wheels. He swung her around in the air while spinning on his feet like a figure skater.

A twenty-year-old philosophy student from the University of Copenhagen missed his father, who had died of sudden unexplained coronary failure. They chose one of the more abstract models: A ball of diverse equipment, which rolled away from the lab while ruffling the hair of the son with a diverse array of instruments, emerging from the surface at regular intervals.

A businessman had lost his wife, who had loved life, wine, and travel as much as he did. She received a humanoid model equipped with booster rockets and retractable arm-wings, allowing her to fly for short distances like a flying squirrel. They climbed to the roof of the building and took off, all the while discussing their future adventures.

The variety of armors dazzled me. In my memory, they blurred together into surreal gestalts. All the suits carried the logo of Birk Industries: A bident growing from a beaker.

"This is only the beginning," said Doctor Birk. "With non-corporeal pilots, the designs are limited only by our imaginations. It may even be possible to create compound armor comprising several smaller armors, individual spirits coordinated by a strong-willed controller."

Soon, repurposed power armor filled the streets. Deceased parents, spouses, children, and friends stretched iridescent arms in the sun and conversed with synthetic voices. Most had learned to adjust the volume by now. The noise complaints had caused City Hall to threaten action.

Money poured into the company coffers, and my salary grew exponentially. Perhaps I could upgrade Maria with rocket boosters, and the three of us could go on a trip?

While preparing to close shop for the day, my phone rang. Sara. I smiled and picked up.

"They took her!" Her voice shook. "I'm sorry…"

"What are you talking… Never mind, I'm coming home."

Sara waited for me on the front lawn, looking dejected. A black government Cadillac lay upside-down on the street, windows smashed and wheels pointing toward the sky, like a black turtle stuck on its back.

"What happened? Where's Maria?"

"They took her! That lady with the eyepatch and a small army of suits. Maria tried to fight them off, but they had some device that disabled the armor. I'm sorry, I didn't know what to do."

Vestergaard picked up after the first ring. "Mr. Vinther. I've been expecting your call."

"Where's my wife, bitch," I said through clenched teeth.

Dr. Vestergaard's voice was calm and consistent. "Your wife is fine, Mr. Vinther. If only you had taken my offer, you would be up to date with the operation. Why don't you visit me at the Ministry? I'll tell the guards to let you through."

"Waitaminute," I shouted, but the line was already dead.

The doctor also picked up immediately. "Kristian," he said. "Are you okay?"

"They took my wife," I yelled.

"You're not the only one. The lab has been inundated with calls from angry customers. I knew Vestergaard would try to sabotage my work!"

"She invited me to visit."

He snorted. "Typical divide and conquer strategy; still trying to turn you against me. You'll have to go alone. The guards won't let me through."

***

The Ministry of Esoteric Development was located on a hilltop outside Copenhagen, with a nice city view. Rumor was the location was intended to prevent esoteric energies from leaking into the city proper. Several concentric circles of electrified fencing surrounded the building. Rumor was this was to keep things in, not out. A narrow gravel path led up the hill to the sole gate in the outer fence. Rumor was that the budget hadn't included any infrastructure funding.

The gravel crunched under my feet as I navigated the winding path toward the gate. The setting sun made the sky glow with orange light, and the air had a faint smell of ozone.

The gate slowly and creakily swung open as I approached.

I followed the winding path through the fences to the front door. Vestergaard's assistant waited with his clipboard, leaning against a large sign. Luminescent letters spelled "Enirejo." He scribbled a note on the board. "Follow me, sir."

Labyrinthine corridors soon caused me to lose all sense of direction. As we went by, people in lab coats stared, and I could hear machinery noise from behind the walls. Signs on doors said "Kafejo," "Robotejo," "Kukejo."

The clipboard man opened a beige door labeled "Estrino" and pushed me inside. Dr. Vestergaard sat behind a long mahogany desk covered with books, papers, and circular coffee stains. A large window on the opposite wall provided a view of a rectangular forest at the bottom of Ministry Hill. The twilight left the office in partial darkness, but Vestergaard was lit by a small, bright desk lamp. She had replaced her lab coat with a pinstripe suit.

She smiled, and her teeth sparkled like piano keys. "Good evening. Glad you could make it."

There were no other chairs, so I took a few steps toward the desk. "Where's my wife?"

She stood. "Direct. I like that. Let's take a trip."

She reached under her desk, and a pneumatic hiss came from behind. When I turned, a section of the wall had disappeared, revealing a white corridor containing a vehicle resembling a golf cart. The cart produced a faint electric buzzing as we rode down the corridor until we emerged into a large hall. A suit of power armor waited in the center; with a gasp, I recognized the homeless man's son.

The head of the armor turned toward us, and I could not help but imagine the child working the controls inside. The tank treads were still.

"Good evening, William," said Vestergaard. "You know

Kristian."

"Good evening, miss," said the armor. "Can I see my dad soon?"

She smiled her sparkling smile again. "Very soon," she said. "Let's show Kristian what you can do."

I followed her gaze and saw that the left half of the hall had been converted into a military training course. Pale yellow sand covered the floor, along with a handful of small, circular huts with conical thatched roofs.

Sandbags and barbed wire surrounded the mock village, and training automatons patrolled the area with machine guns. They looked like crash test dummies and walked as if controlled by a drunk puppeteer.

Vestergaard pointed toward the largest hut. "If you can take out the command hut, I'll call your dad. It's like a game!"

I watched in horror as the armor rolled into the fake desert environment, leaving tracks in the sand behind.

"You're using him as a child soldier!"

She rolled her eyes. "Oh, please, you're talking about an unaging spirit. The child would be twenty-three today."

A jerky automaton guard fired at the armor, but the bullets ricocheted off the surface, tiny sparks the only proof the guns weren't shooting blanks.

"For god's sake, can't you use AI drivers?"

"Of course not. Have you forgotten Ditka's law? 'Any artificial intelligence sufficiently advanced to serve man will eventually refuse to do so.' These spirits have families at home, keeping them loyal. Besides, if the armor is destroyed, the spirit can be re-housed. No one will ever have to die in wars again. We can recycle the extant casualties!"

The armor continued, and the automaton guard fell underneath the treads. Crushed with a screeching sound. The armor tossed the sandbags and barbed wire aside like a bored child discarding old toys.

Dr. Vestergaard smiled at me like a mother trying to calm a hysterical child. "Besides, war is far from the only use for these armored ghosts. Most will be employed in industry, helping to sustain the glorious Danish welfare state."

"Stop trying to distract me," I said. "Where. Is. My. Fucking. Wife."

"She was an aerobics teacher. Her control of the armor is without equal, so she'll train the others. You'll be able to visit regularly. No one is losing access to their loved ones, and they'll feel useful again. Everyone benefits."

"You are treating the dead like tools."

"And you would treat them like commodities. Products to sell for profit. Means to an end either way."

She gave me another card for my collection. "Think about it."

***

It was dark when we returned to the lab, but the light was still on in the doctor's office. He drank coffee from a small porcelain cup, and two more cups waited for us. The scent was sufficient to jolt me awake.

"The place is a fortress," I said. "Even if I made it through, I'd get lost in the labyrinth."

"Yes, a frontal assault is not the solution," said the doctor. "I still haven't found a sufficiently strong-willed spirit for my compound armor design. To make it, we must use trickery."

"You think you're smarter than her?" said Sara from behind, pacing the room like a caged lioness.

He shook his head. "I may be arrogant, but not that much.

What I have over her is an appreciation for the importance of allies. Many heads are better than one."

A knock at the door.

"Case in point," said the doctor. "Come in."

The door opened, and Martin, the homeless man, entered. He threw a pamphlet on the desk. "From the welfare state," he said. "They say I can apply for permission to visit my son." His voice shook with barely contained fury.

More allies soon arrived.

There was old Mrs. Peterson, quiet strength visible in her unfaltering gaze. Losing her husband again had filled her with determination.

The philosophy student arrived shortly afterward. He was tall and thin as a reed and dressed in a beige tweed jacket. He carried a small dark blue Fjällräven backpack and smelled of dust.

The businessman arrived last, as the rest of us discussed our plans. He was a short, plump man, but a plumpness that implied momentum, like a cannonball. You got the sense that once he started, nothing could stop him. He smelled of wine, but it was good wine, and he mostly seemed sober. The strong coffee straightened him up.

We stayed up most of the night, making plans.

***

Once more, I walked the gravelly path to the Ministry building on the hill. Clouds obscured the sun, and the air was cool. I glimpsed the contours of an omni-dog watching from the shadows nearby.

The man with the clipboard waited for me. "I knew you'd be back," he said.

"You can talk, then?"

"Of course. I prefer to listen. I'm John Dahl, Doctor Birk's previous postdoc. I suspect we'll be working together soon."

"Isn't it humiliating to follow her around all the time?"

He laughed. "Are you kidding? I'm next in line; I need to know everything. You'll do well to follow my example."

"Why a clipboard? Why not a hand computer?"

He scribbled. "The tactile notetaking process stimulates the brain and grounds one in material reality. Why do you think the ghosts are so crazy about piloting these armors? Same principle."

***

"Right on time," said Vestergaard when I entered the "Estrino" office. Her impeccable nails drummed on the surface of the desk. "The contract is ready. As soon as you sign, you can see your wife."

I leaned against my side of the desk, looking down at her. "Let's negotiate the terms. It isn't enough that I get to see Maria. My friends need to see their loved ones as well."

She tilted her head to the side and scanned my face with her eye. "Your 'friends'?"

"Yes, I have made friends with several of our customers. That's natural when you reunite people with their loved ones."

"How many friends are we talking about, exactly?"

"Four to begin with."

She shrugged. "Fine, your four friends can see their ghosts as well. You'll be responsible for their actions."

She retrieved a small stack of papers from a drawer and pushed them toward me, along with a silvern pen.

"Conditional on your signature, of course."

I signed.

Vestergaard scanned the signed contract with a hand scanner and returned the physical papers to the drawer. She rose from the chair and shook my hand. "Welcome to the team, Mr. Vinther! You'll find contributing to human welfare far more rewarding than what you've been doing so far."

We rode the cart through a dizzying web of tunnels, past workers in lab coats or suits, most riding similar carts. Sometimes the tunnel intersected smaller hallways where people walked or rode electric scooters. Many carried clipboards.

We arrived in a hall about the size of a grade school gym. A dozen suits of armor moved in complex formations at one side. One suit stood apart from the others and barked instructions. Maria. They were dancing.

Dr. Vestergaard honked the horn on the cart, and the armors froze, forming a metallic tableau. Vestergaard clapped. "Excellent job, Maria. You have a visitor!"

Maria turned, froze for a second, and then covered the distance to the cart in a few gracious bounds.

"Kristian!" she said. "What took you so long?"

I smiled at her burnished visage and imagined her face. "I had to sign a contract before they would let me in. We'll be working together from now on." I turned to Vestergaard. "Excuse me, can I be alone with my wife?"

"No."

Can't blame a guy for trying. The hard way, then. I pushed buttons on the tiny remote in my pocket with no visible results, but inside the armor, I knew the lights on the control board were blinking.

The head of the armor moved slightly; a nod.

We exchanged pleasantries, but the lack of privacy made

deeper communication impossible. I worked the remote.

After a few minutes, Vestergaard looked up and smiled. "As you see, your wife is quite happy. She's exercising her talents, helping new spiritual pilots improve their precision motor skills."

"Why not give Kristian the grand tour?" said Maria. "He can meet his friends, and he'll feel better once he understands the great work we are doing here."

Vestergaard folded her hands behind her head and looked at the ceiling. "Very well. I suppose he'll have to see the place eventually."

***

Dahl waited for us back in the office. He held a silver tray supporting a majestic ball wrapped in tinfoil.

Vestergard sniffed. "What's that smell?"

Dahl put the tray down on the table. "Your girlfriend brought you this, Mr. Vinther. She says it's your favorite dish."

I unwrapped the tinfoil and savored the aroma. The beautiful, yellow Keshi Yena crowned the desk.

"I hope you like strong cheese," said Dahl, retreating from the desk. "And strong spice. Even the omni-dog refused to go anywhere near that thing."

Vestergard rolled her eyes and held her nose. "I'll leave you to your dinner while I prepare your friends."

***

First, we visited the student, Mr. Andersen, and his father-ball, which rolled through a vast hall filled with every type of construction material. Tools emerged, moved, and rotated on the metallic surface as the ball described intricate patterns. Complex edifices seemed to grow from the floor, like a timelapse video of a forest.

The ball stopped before me, and a speaker appeared on the surface. We exchanged idle words while I worked the remote, and Vestergaard tapped on her tablet's screen.

Old Mr. Peterson skated through an obstacle course, dodging projectiles and knocking down automatons. I had to borrow a pair of roller skates and follow along. Using the remote while skating was challenging, but he got the gist.

I rode on William's shoulder, taking down automatons with a beanbag Kalashnikov while Vestergaard applauded. He was too young to be entrusted with the entire plan but agreed to follow instructions.

The businessman's wife practiced flying in a massive mechanical aviary with many other flight-capable models. Some had jetpacks, some transformed into planes, and some could fly for no discernible reason. She used her boosters to glide from treetop to treetop while I held on for dear life.

"I hope you had a good time with your friends," said Vestergaard while the cart zoomed through the labyrinth. Dahl scribbled beside her.

I pushed the barrel of my gun into her neck, and her body jerked from the shock. "Stop at the next intersection."

Vestergaard drew a sharp breath. The sound of scribbling stopped as Dahl turned, his eyes growing wide. The cart decelerated, and I grabbed the side to avoid losing balance.

"What. Do you think. You are doing," hissed Vestergaard from between clenched teeth.

"Where on god's green earth did you get a gun," said Dahl, nearly shouting. "No real weapons ever make it in here. The omni-dog makes sure of…"

He sniffed the air, and his eyes grew wider as he recognized the aroma.

"Yes," I said. "We used sufficiently strong spice and sufficiently old cheese to ensure even the omni-dog would not be able to detect it."

The cart stopped, and an eerie silence descended upon the corridor. I kept the gun steady, and my eyes darted between Vestergaard and Dahl.

"This is pointless," said Vestergaard. "What on earth is your goal here? To abscond with your wife? You'll spend the rest of your life on the run! You can't accomplish anything by yourself."

"That is true," I said, and then I heard the drill.

The sound echoed through the hall, vibrations causing my teeth to clatter, and pieces of plaster fell from the roof.

The wall next to us crumbled like a slow-motion explosion, pieces of plaster and concrete flying through the air and rolling across the floor. The robotic ball containing the late Mr. Andersen swept through the hole and landed in front of the cart. The drill returned to the ball, and a pair of speakers emerged in its place.

"Good evening, young man," said the metallic voice of the inhabitant. "I'm happy you made our meeting."

Vestergaard laughed. "I did not see that coming. Still, it makes no difference. I already triggered the alarm, and an old man in a ball will be no match for our security. Abandon this foolish endeavor, and I'll subtract the cost of the wall from your sign-up bonus."

The sound of boots on concrete echoed from around the corner.

"Let's roll," I said to the ball, and the ball rolled. It stopped next to the cart, and a small shelf emerged. I jumped onto the shelf and grabbed hold of a handle that appeared at just the right height. Vestergaard looked at me with disdain; Dahl scribbled.

The ball sped down the hall while the shelf stayed in place. Half a dozen security guards blocked our progress as we rounded the corner. They wore impeccable uniforms and covered their faces with dark helmets. Electricity sparkled from stun batons.

"Drop the gun!" shouted the leader.

We zoomed toward the guards, who formed an orderly line blocking the corridor, brandishing stun batons. As we came within arm's reach, a series of metal rods emerged from the bottom of the ball and spun around the axis, knocking the guards from their feet and sending them spinning through the air.

The corridor opened into an empty hall about the size of a soccer field. A larger group of guards blocked the exit on the opposite side, too many to knock aside. I looked back and saw a similar group getting into position behind us.

A feedback whine sounded from a hidden loudspeaker, followed by Vestergaard's voice: "You've had your fun. It's not too late."

"Send the signal," I said to the ball.

For a few minutes, all was quiet, each side waiting for the other to make a move. A faint droning sound came from behind the soldiers facing us, like wheels on concrete.

A glint of light from gleaming metal. Mr. Peterson's lean body burst through the open door on skating wheels, knees bent, weaving between the disoriented guards like a wheeled ballerina, knocking them over like bowling pins.

The guards milled around, some shouting ignored orders. Open paths between them formed and disappeared. The ball accelerated, and I held on as we rushed into one of the paths. We moved through a shifting labyrinth of opportunities and then through the door into a narrower corridor.

The corridor widened, and we found ourselves in a desert, sunlight shining from the artificial sky above. The air was warm and dry, and I blinked against the light.

When my vision returned, an army of automatons blocked our way. They marched from a mock village, spilling from the small huts like clowns from a clown car. Like a single unit, they lowered their rifles.

The ball moved from side to side. Dozens of rifles fired, and I heard metal striking the side like hail. The ball halted, I lost my grip, flew over the handle, and landed in the sand.

I spat sand from my bleeding mouth and waited for the impact of the bullets. Nothing. All was quiet in the desert.

I raised my head and saw the ball unmoving in the sand. The bullets stuck to the side like magnets, and the automatons had frozen in position.

"You can get up now," said the voice of Vestergaard from the sky. "The soldiers won't harm you. Exit through the small door in the side, and we can work this out."

I got on my feet and brushed the sand off my clothes.

"Time to play, William," I said.

The sound of an engine coming to life emerged behind the mock village.

"What are you doing, William," said Vestergaard. "This is not a game. Let the adults handle things!"

Roaring fire engulfed one of the huts and two nearby automatons. I smiled as the heat reached my face. The hut burned away, straw floating in all directions on waves of hot air. Tank treads crushed what remained as William emerged from the fire, flamethrower making short work of several more nearby automatons.

The remains of the mechanical army turned toward this new threat. Bullets ricocheted off the armor without effect, and the treads crushed those who escaped the flames.

"Can we see my dad now?" asked William.

A sigh came from the loudspeaker. "Fine. Go ahead and leave. It's not like there's anywhere for you to go."

William raised his flamethrower arm and sprayed a fire fountain into the air. I climbed onto his back, careful not to burn my hands on hot metal.

We drove through the gates blocking the exit, metal doors crumbling like aluminum. The remaining guards scattered at our approach, and the loudspeakers were silent. We smashed through the front doors, glass raining around us like sharp hailstones. I got a few cuts, but nothing major. The taste of blood on my lips invigorated me.

Real soldiers surrounded the building, carrying real weapons. Armored vehicles blockaded the path, and a black helicopter lazily drifted from side to side in the air like a bored humming bee. Even with all the armors at my disposal, this would have been one hell of a fight.

"Where's my dad?" asked William.

"On the other side, I'm afraid," I replied.

A tank approached, followed by soldiers. I started raising my hands in surrender.

Sleek metal shot past me, followed by a trail of smoke, struck the tank dead on, and exploded into a fireball. I closed my eyes against the heat and light.

When I opened them, the tank had stopped moving, and the front was twisted and charred. The soldiers had scattered and retreated toward their comrades. I turned my head. Maria. A bazooka adorned her right arm.

A shout from the roof of the building. I saw the plump businessman waving at us from above with a big smile. His wife next to him, arm-wings unfolded. I imagined her smile.

"We're going to get help," he shouted. "We can't beat them directly, but the public won't stand for this. I know it!"

He climbed onto the back of his late wife.

"Wait!" I shouted. "What if they shoot you down?"

"They won't shoot at a civilian. Don't worry about me; I'm too rich to fall!"

His wife took several steps back, ran forward, and jumped from the roof, arms out-spread. The booster rockets roared, and the couple gained altitude. When they were far above the army of soldiers, the rockets cut out, and they glided toward the city.

A few soldiers raised their rifles, but no one fired. The helicopter let them pass.

"Very nice," said the voice of Vestergaard from behind me. "You must be proud of all the commotion you've caused."

William rotated until we both faced her. She was sweaty, her hair ruffled, and she looked annoyed. Her hand held a cell phone. "Call the doctor," she said. "Tell him it's over."

I sighed, reached for the phone, twisted my arm at the last second, and tore the patch from the hidden, sensitive eye, snapping the string.

Sunlight glinted from exposed glass. Vestergaard screamed. Her bionic eye looked at me for a split second - electric pupil dilated and blinking - before her hand snapped up to cover it. I swept her legs from under her.

Dahl dropped the clipboard and threw his pencil at me with a flick of the wrist. Pain in my shielding palm as the razor sharp tip penetrated. Dahl rammed me as I tore it out, and we fell to the ground together. I kneed him in the groin; he punched me in the face.

He pinned me to the ground. Something long and sharp dangling in front of my face. Instinctively, I grabbed, stabbing behind me. A yell of pain. The pressure eased.

I stood and saw Dahl lying on the ground, his face twisted in pain. A pencil was planted in his leg, still attached to the clipboard with a piece of string. Blood stained his hand.

Vestergaard had managed to locate her eyepatch and was holding it in place with her hand, getting to her feet.

I pulled the pencil from Dahl's leg and held it against Vestergaard's neck, pulling her up. "STAND DOWN," I yelled.

The soldiers stopped their approach. The helicopter drifted like a leaf caught in a breeze. "Get out of here," I said to William. "Find your dad. I'll be fine." He drove down the hill, and the soldiers stood aside to let him pass.

Vestergaard laughed, and the pencil tip drew a single drop of blood.

"What's so funny?" I asked.

"This is perfect. I couldn't ask for a better scene than the two of us at the top of the hill, you threatening to slash my neck with a pencil. The media will have a field day with this!"

I gripped the pencil tighter. "What're you on about? Don't try anything funny."

"You think those soldiers are here to shoot you? In Denmark? Those rifles aren't even loaded. They're witnesses. We're filming this."

"You're messing with my head. We escaped."

"Yes, and what a daring escape it was! Exciting chases, technicolor combat with teams of security guards, explosions! You demonstrated the dangers of unfettered spirits far more effectively than any argument I could make. Procuring a higher budget and more regulations will be a breeze."

Dahl took the pencil from my hand without resistance, and Vestergaard slipped from my grip.

"We did not predict everything," she continued. "The plan was to catch you all here. Still, a few armors making their way into the city will only turn public opinion more fervently toward poltergeist control. Mr. Dahl has been taking copious notes on your behavioral patterns, and I daresay he got close."

Behind me, the scribbling of the pen on the clipboard resumed, ink mixed with blood.

"Why don't you call the doctor?" she said. "Once the new laws pass, Birk Industries will be nationalized. Let's have dinner and discuss the terms. I don't know about you, but I'm starving! … What?"

She followed my gaze toward the city. Pillars of smoke rose from several neighborhoods in the distance.

"Jesus Christ," said Vestergaard. "The local authorities should be able to handle a few armors!"

I laughed. "A few? The doctor has released all the armors from his lab and any spirit willing to take one. Hell is empty and…"

She was already too far away to appreciate my erudition. The helicopter picked her up, and the army followed down the hill.

***

Armors were everywhere in the city, stomping on cars, uprooting trees, enjoying their newfound physicality. I swerved the car to avoid them and careened through cluttered streets, looking for recognizable figures. Perhaps I could talk some sense into Vestergaard. Find a compromise.

A tree fell across the street, and I stomped on the brakes, twisted the wheel, and slammed sideways into the trunk, biting my tongue. The seatbelt squeezed the air from my lungs, and blackness swallowed the world.

The taste of metal in my mouth brought me back to my senses. I stepped from the car into the city. The smell of burnt rubber. I shook my head. Helicopters darted across the sky; the cacophony made it hard to focus. Buzzing rotors, glass breaking, steel against concrete.

Farther down the street, a tall suit of armor with four arms brandished a car in each hand. A tank shell exploded at the center of the torso, and the armor fell, pinned underneath the vehicles. Nearby armors suffered similar fates, some swarmed by tanks, others hit by missiles from buzzing helicopters.

A massive tank emerged from behind a corner, and I saw Vestergaard resting her elbows on the edge of the open hatch. Green helmet on her head. She directed the carnage, radio in hand. "Come join us," she yelled to me. "Let's work together to restore order. The job offer is still on the table."

The ground shook, and my teeth clattered. Vestergaard stopped talking and frowned. I turned on my feet.

An enormous suit of armor towered above us. The right hand was clenched into a fist. I blinked against the sunlight and gasped. Not a fist; a ball. A ball full of tools.

The left arm terminated in smoldering booster rockets, and retractable wings had turned into defensive blades.

At the foot of the right leg, William's tank treads supported the massive frame above, flamethrower ready to defend the giant from puny attackers attempting to climb to the top. His arms pointed upward, connecting him with the larger body.

The skating wheels of old Mr. Peterson supported the other leg.

The torso and head were unfamiliar: A box with a smaller box on top, two bright blue spotlights protruding from the upper one. A metallic grating below the spotlights constituted the mouth.

The spotlights flooded the tank with sapphire blue, and the voice of Doctor Birk emerged from the grating: "You will not win so easily, Vestergaard."

The tank turret rotated toward the armor.

"Doctor!" I yelled. "Did you create compound armor pilotable by a living person?"

The spotlights tilted toward me. "Sadly, no, but it's okay. I'll be with my family soon."

The turret stopped, the cannon pointing straight at the metal giant.

"Surrender," said Vestergaard while fastening the straps on her helmet. "We can still negotiate."

"This is not a negotiation. It's a demonstration."

She shrugged and disappeared into the interior of the tank.

I ran. Behind me, the city burned.

***

The grainy clip of Vestergaard's tank somersaulting through the air went viral. I saw it on the news, on the net, in music video edits, and in my dreams. The armors were defeated, but there were no viral videos of that defeat, no music videos of the orderly cleanup. Only the tank spinning across countless screens, through buildings, and into the public imagination.

The parliamentary debates raged for days, every second broadcast live as the wheels of society ground to a halt.

"Our ancestors should be venerated, not exploited," shouted the prime minister, speaking to a crowded legislature, wearing a tan suit. "This recent debacle shows what happens when we forget that the deceased deserve rest and respect after a life of toil. The combined resources of the welfare state barely managed to contain the chaos. This could've made Linköping look like a picnic!

"Therefore, today, we pass the Let Grandma Sleep Act, banning the use of human spirits in any mechanized process. No more robot ghosts!"

Thunderous applause.

***

Vestergaard came to visit the following week. I sat in the garden, enjoying the quiet and the warmth of the evening sun. The buzzing of the bees. She still had a few bruises but was remarkably unscathed, considering her viral flight through the city.

"Evening," I said, not bothering to rise.

She nodded in my direction. "I came to congratulate you. You somehow defeated me without foiling any of my plans."

"We didn't need to change the outcome, only the optics. Doctor Birk understood that. He gave his life to teach you."

Sara came through the front door, carrying a tray. "Oh, hey, doctor. Do you want a glass of lemonade?

Vestergaard shrugged and took a glass from the tray; yellow liquid flowed through the straw. "Indeed. Instead of causing new regulations, you convinced the people that none would ever be sufficient. Years of research down the drain. The whole debacle swept under the carpet with no charges filed. Still, I'm surprised you would sacrifice your wife to teach me a lesson."

She nodded toward the suit of armor standing guard in the middle of the garden, daffodils growing from the grating in the helmet.

"I sacrificed nothing," I said, defiantly drinking my lemonade. Sweet acidity. "Maria is still with us, right here. She may no longer speak, but we can speak to her. The armor is now a shrine instead of a tool or weapon."

"You don't think a statue would be more appropriate?"

"It's the uncanny valley."

Vestergaard raised her half-empty glass in a toast to the silent metal guardian. "Cheers. You chose your side. I hope you're happy with the outcome."

Turning toward me, she flipped another card into my lap. "This is a speed bump. Your previous contract is void, but I can find other work for you."

"I already have several of your cards."

"The act of giving is what matters."

She strode out of the garden, leaving her empty glass in the grass.

Sara and I drank our lemonade while watching the sunset, the evening air cool against our skin. Maria's glass stayed full. A bee landed on the edge but left the contents alone. When the shadows reached our chairs, we went inside to make tea.

***

I woke early in the night. The warmth of Sara's body, the gentle rhythm of her breath. A faint aroma of sweat on clean linen. Still, sleep would not come.

Going for a walk to clear my head, I saw Maria in the moonlight. "Goodnight. Having trouble sleeping as well? Hope I didn't wake you."

I tried to imagine her sleeping body inside, but the image was indistinct.

The taste of fresh air cleared my head. A few minutes later, I emerged from the house again with the old Ouija board I had managed to locate at the back of the cupboard. Placed it at her feet and kneeled. Blades of grass tickled my arms.

Why should I not speak with my wife? Why should the graves be silent while birds sing interminably in the trees? I can talk to philosophers a thousand-year dead through their work, yet I am forbidden all intercourse with one who lived life viscerally, spreading joy every day with her movement across the stage; I will not let words be all that remain while blood turns to dust; if any god or demon wants to enforce these capricious rules, I dare them to seize control.

I looked up at the helmet, trying to meet her gaze.

"Are you happy?"

My fingers on the planchette.

SUBMARINE SALVATION

The submarine cannot sail
through a frozen lake
in an underground cave.

The pilot peeks from the tower,
climbs onto the steel,
pirouettes across the ice,
stopping at the rock.

A bearded man squats
on an outcropping,
brandishing a burly branch
above his rival below.

The winner takes a
hibernating vessel,
stuck to the surface,
interior lights starting to dim.

When the fragrance of spring
thaws the ice,
will anyone be there
to greet the machine?

STARFISH

I compare myself to a starfish,
Five senses like five arms.
When I revolve, I scent the
Constellations, hear the flowers, taste
The mooing of the cows, touch
The fragrance of the grass,
Perceive the music of the spheres.

I roll across fields to
The city, savoring each scene
With pentacled perception. Lights
Have the pungent odor of ozone,
A freshness constructed, not grown.
I hear citizens move across
Predetermined paths, taste their ambition.

In the centre,
The tower holds.
The lynchpin of civilization,
Glass and chrome connecting

Heaven and earth. The lobby devoid
Of life, only guards. Rolling between
Their legs. Elevator muzak like popcorn.
The engine in the basement roars.

The tower launches, incinerating
The city below.
Five arms attach to five controls.
I ride the pillar of smoke
Towards celestial awe.

APOEQUORIN

The jellyfish is eating my memories.
It caught me while swimming, wrapping
translucent tentacles around my skull.
I only remember one parent, two of
my former homes, and half my cat.
I did not know that they could do that.
I claw at wet tentacles, but they
slip through my fingers like
cold cup noodles.
I shout for it to stop, choking
on saltwater.
Did I ever have parents?
What color was my cat?
Where do I live?
My shouts go unheeded;
jellyfish do not have ears.
I stop, breathe, relax, remember
the jellyfish.
My dad was a jellyfish.
Took me fishing, using tentacles

as fishing poles.
"Why are you doing this?" I asked him.
"To protect you."
My pet was a jellyfish.
Stroked its smooth surface while
nematocytes played with my hair.
"Just relax," it said.
"Let it happen."
My childhood home was a jellyfish,
the pulsating bell above
protecting me from the rain.
Alphabet blocks in my room spelled out
"YOU CAN LIVE HERE FOREVER".
I smiled and lay down
on my gastrodermal bed.
Devoid of memories, my body crumples
into the water, like a jellyfish.
The oceans will remember me,
for as long as the currents flow.

ABOUT THE AUTHOR

Simon Christiansen is a writer, poet, and game designer living in Denmark. His stories have been published in a variety of literary journals, and he has written award-winning works of interactive fiction. He is the recipient of three Xyzzy awards for interactive fiction and has been shortlisted for the Niels Klim award for best Danish science fiction novelette.

When not writing, he enjoys reading, juggling, and walking. Visit his website at www.sichris.com.